"Two Doors Down"

By David H. Snyder

Christmas, 2005
Revised, Christmas, 2010

Published by
Gamlewszqvskyicz Press
Filterboro, NC
ISBN 978-0-9894360-2-1

This book is dedicated with great love to my wife Sherry, and to my children; Sarahannah, Sasha, Matthew, and Nicholas, who now know much greater stability than our family once had known: may the spirit of Christmas remain wondrous and magical for all of your lives.

Love, Daddy

1

At age seven, Sarahannah had learned to notice changes in her neighborhood. Having lived in four homes in four different states in her short life, she had not developed a typical childhood perspective, that Neighborhoods Are Forever. Unlike her younger siblings, who simply didn't remember living anywhere else, she didn't name each house on her block for the family that lived within; there was no Blackwell House or Franklin Place. For better or worse, people moved away and other families replaced them.

Nevertheless, the gregarious Sarahannah looked at the neighborhood as "half full" rather than "half empty." It meant the opportunity to meet an infinitely-expanding number of new people and to make new friends.

Yet, there was often a nagging doubt that plagued Sarahannah's thoughts, a kind of worry about the instability of life. After all those moves, she was coming to accept the idea that everything was just as transient as her address. She had become a little unsure about the permanence of anything.

"Mommy," Sarahannah had started one spring morning while they planted sunflower seeds with her sister Sasha along the east side of the house, "Won't we be gone from here before these flowers come out? Why are we doing this?"

Kneeling in the dirt, Mommy stopped and smiled a tired smile that indicated the irony hadn't escaped her, either.

"Honey, don't worry. They'll be blooming before you know it. We don't plan to move away again all that soon."

"But you remember those pumpkin seeds we planted in West Virginia? We never saw them grow up."

"You are right. But we plant things to show we still have faith that they will grow and that we will still be around to enjoy them when they do."

They finished with a hopeful pat of the freshly churned earth. While Mommy watered the small plot, the girls joined Sasha's twin brother Matthew at the Loquat Tree at the edge of the front yard, their neighborhood observation post. For her part, Sasha had no such doubts about the permanence of things: she expected all butterflies to live forever. Matthew was content knowing what he could see and feel.

It was a quiet day. With nothing to observe down the street, the three children rode their bicycles, mostly up and down the driveway, playing small games with their young brother, Nicholas. And in their own fashion, the children observed the world as it went by. On this, their latest home street, there was no sidewalk and precious few other children to play with on the block. That meant they really couldn't go anywhere without their parents, and as the oldest child, Sarahannah was starting to chafe against those restrictions.

The aging oak trees were budding and the rainy skies clearing for the spring when the neighborhood changed, quietly but permanently. The Man moved in two doors down.

Matthew noticed it first while he was out riding his bike.

"Mom, we have new neighbors," he proclaimed. "I wonder if they have any kids," he added, hopefully.

Mom looked up from her cleaning. She had seen a white-bearded, rotund, older man and his rusted, coughing red pickup truck that came straight out of the 1970's television sitcom "Sanford and Son." It wasn't exactly the nicest home in the neighborhood, and now a man who owned a crummy-looking pickup truck was moving in. *A dump and a truck*, she thought. Sounds about right.

Aloud, though, she said, "I'm sure we'll find out soon enough, son."

"We should bring them a pie!" exclaimed Sasha, pushing her blonde, bangy hair out of her eyes and looking up from a coloring book. The five year old had a great capacity to anticipate the wants of others, particularly if it meant she could visit with them. And talk. Sasha was a very outgoing little girl.

Calculating the many chores she had in front of her, Mommy didn't answer about the pie. Sasha kept on.

"We could make an apple pie like Daddy likes and give him a slice and then maybe we could all have some and then give the new neighbors some of what's left over!"

"Or just make a second pie," offered Sarahannah, ever practical.

"Or maybe we could make three pies, because Mr. Phillips likes apple pie, too," Sasha went on, not quite as practical. She would have found reason to start a bakery to serve the entire neighborhood had not Mommy interrupted.

"Sasha, you have a big heart, and wonderful ideas. But every time you think of one, it means more work for me. Let's just start with one pie and we can bring it to the new people in a day or so."

Nicholas softly cried from his bedroom, just awakening from a nap. Dreaming about Florida alligators and Santa Claus, he felt a little frightened. Mommy left the dining room to help him out of his toddler bed and the older kids went outside to play.

Riding their scooters, they were stopped at the end of the driveway by a sight two doors down. A man was lifting objects out of the bed of the pickup truck, and hauling them into the house.

"There he is!" shouted Sasha.

"Shhh, Sashie. Not so loud," warned Sarahannah. She wanted to watch without being noticed. They ducked behind an overgrown hedge.

"Do you see any kids?" wondered Matthew, peering through the bush. He hoped to make some new friends.

Sarahannah looked. The man pulled a lamp out of the truck and carried it through the trees in the front yard and into the garage. He walked with a heavy but determined step, and kept his eyes in front of him the entire way. The children waited for what felt like an hour, but only three or four minutes later the man emerged once again and walked back to the truck. He paused for a moment to rub his expansive belly, seemingly contemplating his next move.

"He looks too old to have kids," Sarahannah observed, as much to herself as to her siblings.

"He has a beard!" shouted Sasha, laughing. "Just like that man at Daddy's work. I remember how rough it felt. It was just like sandpaper and when ..."

"Sasha, be quiet!" warned Matthew. Sarahannah looked at Sasha while turning her back to the man. "No one is helping him. I wonder if he's alone."

"If he's lonely, maybe we should bring him a pie," said Sasha. "We could be his friend."

"I wish he had kids. Then we could be friends with them," answered Matthew.

Nicholas came outside, comforted

by a chocolate chip cookie from Mommy. His Florida alligator dream had been forgotten. He was agile for a toddler, and climbed on his tricycle to join his brother and sisters.

"Whud-doin, Sissie?" he asked Sarahannah once he reached the oldest child. The kids looked like they were hiding.

"Nothing, Nicky. Stay back from the road," warned Sarahannah. She was learning to take responsibility for her little brother, but Mommy said she still needed to learn not to be bossy about it. Nicholas had a bit of chocolate smeared on his cheek but Sarahannah decided not to say anything about it. Instead, she returned her attention to their new neighbor.

The bearded man pulled a desk chair out of the bed, and rolled it inside the house. Still no one else appeared in his yard. When he returned, he seemed to stop for a moment--not exactly looking down the street at the kids--but they ducked away anyhow. That's when he lifted out a big round bag from the truck.

"Look!" exclaimed Sasha. "It's beautiful!"

It was an unusual sight to the

children. The biggest bags they had ever seen came from the department store when Mommy or Daddy took them shopping for clothes. But those were plastic, and were recycled as garbage bags soon after. The bag the bearded man carried seemed to be made from some soft material, maybe velvet, and was colored a rich burgundy, and pulled closed with a gold cord. You'd never throw away a bag like that. Unlike before, the man lowered this object to the ground before toting it inside. The bag seemed heavy, and the contents shifted when it came down.

The attention of all the children, including little Nicholas, was riveted on the bag. The man loosened the cord and peered inside, rummaging through its contents. He seemed intent on his search, but a quick glance their way sent the children scurrying back up the driveway; they'd been seen.

"Go back, Sasha, and see what he's doing," directed Sarahannah, once they were safe inside the garage.

"No way! I'm not going down there alone!" Sasha answered.

"No way!" mimicked Nicholas.

"I'm staying up here in the yard," announced Matthew.

"You can just sneak down along the bushes, Sash--it'll be alright," Sarahannah tried, a little unconvincingly. Sasha simply folded her arms and shook her head.

Climbing on her bike, the older sister formed a quick plan.

"Okay. Well, if you won't go, I'll get on my bike and pretend to just ride around. Then maybe I'll go by and see what's in the bag," she announced.

"Wait! We'll go with you," Sasha yelled, running for her bike.

It went just as the seven year old planned. With a small head start, Sarahannah mounted her purple bicycle and slowly pedaled down the driveway toward the road. Once she could hear Sasha catching up on her bike--guided by a rattling pair of training wheels--Sarahannah swiftly made a U-turn, watching her younger sister shoot by all the way to the edge of the street.

"Hey!" yelled Sasha, braking. She finally came to a stop just before going into the street. Matthew laughed. Sasha couldn't quite control her bike as well as she would like.

"Now that you're down there, just look and see what the man is doing," demanded Sarahannah in a stage whisper from further up the driveway. Nicholas had stopped next to her on his tricycle and watched through the hedge.

Sasha didn't like the trick, but looked anyways. "I don't see anything," she reported. "Except some boxes wrapped up like presents!"

"Presents?" wondered Sarahannah.

"Chri-mas presents!" shouted Nick.

Sasha joined her siblings back up the driveway. "Presents--you know, gifts. You can see them from here," she pointed out.

The children looked. Sure enough, at the junction of the man's driveway and the street, under his mailbox, they could see four gaily decorated packages.

"What are they, Sissy?" asked Sasha.

"I don't know."

"Are they for us?" Sasha pressed.

"I'm sure of it." Matthew analyzed everything carefully, and his considered opinion was actually highly regarded by the older kids. That settled the matter.

"I'd like a present," Sarahannah added, thinking to herself. "Even if it's not my birthday."

"Present! Chri-mas present!" chanted Nicholas. He started rolling his trike down the driveway. The older children were preoccupied with speculating about the presents before they realized the small child had left them. He made it to the road before they could start after him. Turning into the street, Nicholas made a beeline for the boxes. His head start on his siblings disappeared quickly, but he made it to the front of Mr. Phillips' house next door before they could catch him.

"Nicky!" Sarahannah said, with some exasperation. She grabbed the handlebar of his trike. "You can't leave the driveway! You'll get in trouble or get hurt. Turn around and come back home," she instructed.

But Nicholas was stubborn when it came to the potential of sweets and presents. "No!" he said determinedly. He tried to peddle.

Sarahannah worked to turn him around. While they struggled, Sasha and Matthew took the opportunity to go forward to the bearded man's house. On their bikes they clattered up to the small pile of presents. Sasha glanced at the one on top.

"Sissy! They're for us!" she exclaimed excitedly. "Our names are on them! Look, 'Matthew,' 'Sarahannah,' 'Nicholas,'... and 'Sasha! That's me!" Matthew jumped off his bike and lifted the present with his name on it. Even the prospect of a gift, however, failed to appeal to Sarahannah's growing sense of danger. "Matthew! Sasha! Come back right now before we get in trouble with Mommy. Don't let that man catch you touching his stuff."

The twins re-mounted their bikes and started to wheel away, slowly. It's hard to ride a bike while looking backward.

"Why can't we have the presents?" Sasha asked, admiring the packages. A tear was forming in her eye.

"Because they aren't ours. They belong to the new man. And we are in the street!" added her older sister, with authority. She took charge now. "If we don't get back home right now, we're going to get in big trouble."

This time, even Nicholas turned back. All four children made it back to the driveway, and with one last look at the mysterious pile of presents, they entered the garage on their way into the house. As they opened the door from the garage into the kitchen, all four heard a happy, deep, rolling guttural laughter float down the street...sounding something like, "Ho, ho, ho!"

The children looked at each other.

"Was that something on TV?" Matthew asked.

"Let's ask Mommy," Sasha replied.

Before they could turn the doorknob to enter, however, Nicholas blurted out a name that sent quick chills running up and down their spines.

"Santa! Santa! Santa!" Nicky exclaimed.

"Shhhhh!" scolded Matt. "Let's go inside."

"I was just coming out to check on you," Mommy told them as they entered. "What were you doing out there?"

"Presents!" shouted Nicholas. "Chri-mas presents, Mommy!"

"What's that, Nicky?" Mommy asked. "What about 'presents'?"

"Santa!" He added.

"Oh, he's just talking about a game we were playing," answered Sarahannah, quickly. She had decided not to let Mommy in on the secret, for now, anyway. "We were pretending that Santa Claus was bringing us presents." Matthew and Sasha said nothing, so Mommy accepted the explanation.

But Nicholas got mad.

"Presents, Mommy!" he shouted again, becoming demanding. "Presents!"

Mommy answered soothingly, "Yes, Nicky. When Christmas comes--or your birthday--there will be lots of presents."

"Presents!" Nicholas answered again, more in frustration at his lack of verbal skills. He didn't lack expression in other areas, and ended up throwing a screaming fit on the floor. Mommy picked him up and trucked him back to his bed, where he alternately hollered and sat in wonder over the whole affair.

Meanwhile, the other children went to the girls' bedroom. Sarahannah shut the door. Sasha bombarded her with questions.

"Sissy! Why did you say that? We weren't pretending! Why didn't you tell Mommy? Why didn't we pick up the presents? What are we going to do now?"

"Should we tell Mom?" asked Matthew. There was no answer, for the moment.

"Maybe Santa really did bring those presents," responded Sarahannah, as much to herself as her sister.

"What do you mean?" wondered Sasha. But she quickly answered her own question. "You mean that man down the street is Santa Claus?"

Matthew analyzed the facts.

"Well, he has a white beard and he kind of looks like Santa. And he left presents with our names on them. How did he know our names?" he asked.

"Why would Santa live here on our street?" added Sasha. "He lives at the North Pole. And I didn't see any elves helping him unpack his truck. Where are the elves?"

It was a good point. She continued, "And I didn't see any reindeer. Did you?"

"I'm not sure," Sarahannah answered, thoughtfully.

Mommy appeared in the doorway of the bedroom the girls shared, carrying Nicholas, who looked tired. His eyes were red from crying. His tantrum had worn him out, but he hadn't forgotten about the presents.

"I'm going to put Nick-nack down for a nap, everybody. I want you to quiet down and start getting ready for one, too."

The children normally fussed about taking a nap. Each had a lot on her mind this day, however, and they were preoccupied as they went through the motions of clearing the toys off their beds to make room to lie down. Matthew joined Nick in the boys' room, leaving the girls alone.

They didn't say a word until after Mommy tucked them in and closed the blinds. The mid-afternoon sunshine was suddenly eclipsed by clouds, adding to their plaintive attitude.

"Do you really think he's Santa, Sissy?" asked Sasha again, whispering this time.

Sarahannah wanted to believe. It was incredible to imagine Kris Kringle moving into their neighborhood, but it all just seemed to add up.

Sasha was curious. She asked the questions, because at age five she was more inclined to believe in Santa than her older sister. She couldn't shake the image of Saint Nick living and working at the North Pole. Her thoughts changed direction, though, when she imagined being friends with the Great Man, helping the elves make toys, petting the reindeer and watching them fly. She thought of the enormous velvet sack, and the presents--one of which with her name on it--that had seemingly emerged from it. She imagined what was inside her package. Even at her age, Sasha knew she shared her name with few other children. The box in the green wrapping paper with a red bow must be for her! What was inside it? Oh, how she wished she'd picked it up, just to get a feel for it. Sasha pictured herself hefting the present, getting a feel for it, shaking it ever so slightly. As she started to pull off the paper, in her mind's eye, she finally drifted off to sleep.

Meanwhile, Matthew was having a tough time concentrating on anything in the bedroom he shared with Nicholas. Once he latched on to an idea, the younger brother was a terrier--with dogged determination, he wouldn't let it go.

"Matt-ew...Matt-ew...Matt-ew...wudat Santa Claus? Matt-ew?"

Eventually, Matthew knew he had to respond, even if only to stop the onslaught.

"I don't know why he would live on our street, Nicholas. But it might be." That left even Nicholas something to think about--quietly. As excited as they were, the two boys soon drifted off.

2

It didn't seem that more than a few minutes went by before Sarahannah was shaking Sasha awake.

"Sashie! Wake up! Santa has been here! We have presents!"

With the mists of dreamland still heavy in her head, Sasha couldn't fathom what was happening. Christmas? Was it Christmas? Snow on the ground? No one had told her Christmas was coming. How could Santa have come without Christmas? And then she remembered the bearded neighbor and the presents at the foot of his driveway.

Sasha pushed back the blankets, and ran out to the living room at full steam.

Matthew was examining four gift-wrapped boxes. Mommy looked like she was trying to figure out where they came from. Nicholas didn't seem sure what was going on and Sarahannah added to the confusion by jumping around.

"Santa's been here! He lives just down the street! And he brought us presents!"

"Yay!!" exclaimed Sasha, still unsure of everything. Then she spied the green box with the red bow sitting in her living room, Mommy stooped over it, wonderingly.

"It has your names on the packages," she said to the children. To herself, she added, "They were left on the front porch. I would have thought the mail carrier would have delivered them to us, but there's no address on them. Just your names on little cards." Then she thought of something Sarahannah had said; alarm bells rang loud in her head.

"Sarahannah, what did you mean when you said Santa lives down the street?"

The seven year old stopped jumping. She had said too much in her excitement. She half turned away from Mommy, towards her own package. She studied the name tag, which simply read "Sarahannah" in careful black ink calligraphy.

"Sarahannah?" Mommy asked again.

Her daughter paused again, then looked up.

"Nothing, Mommy. Like I said, we were pretending. We pretended the new family next door to Mr. Phillips was Santa and Mrs. Claus and they had elves." She didn't need to embellish the story, but it seemed much better if they really had seen elves earlier.

"Chri-mas presents," offered Nicholas.

"But these presents don't look like presents that came from the store," pronounced Matthew.

"Why do you say, that, Matty?" Mommy asked.

Matthew studied the packages for another moment. "They look old-fashioned. The wrapping paper feels soft and thick, and it doesn't have one of those press-on bows on top."

"That's very smart of you to notice, Matt. I think you might have something there," replied Mommy. "But, we still don't know where they came from."

"Can we open the presents, Mommy?" Sasha asked.

"No, honey. We don't know what they are for, or who they came from really, and I want to talk with Daddy about it."

Groans from the children. Mommy found a spot in the closet for the presents. Out of sight, out of mind, she hopefully thought to herself, and moved back towards her work at the computer.

"That doesn't mean you can't pretend about Santa and Christmas," she told the kids. "I want you to leave that new neighbor alone, though, until we've had a chance to meet him." "We" being, of course, the adults.

Matthew, ever the explorer, headed outside to look around. Who knows what clues he could develop by observing the new neighbor's house, and perhaps, the new neighbor himself.

While he took up a position along the hedge, his sisters stepped out the door to kill some time outdoors while waiting for Daddy to come home. Just then, the children caught a flash of someone speeding by on a bike. Blurred in the image, along with a red bicycle, yellow sun dress and long, brown hair...was a gift-wrapped box!

"Jessica! Jessica!" Sasha and Sarahannah shouted together, running to the road after their friend. Jessica was in third grade. She lived across the street and four doors down, the opposite direction of the new neighbor. Ignoring Sasha and Sarahannah, she pedaled as hard as she could into her driveway, and in a deft motion, hopped off the tottering bike and ran into her house, package still in tow.

"Why didn't she stop?" wondered Sasha, staring after Jessica.

"Girls... ." Matthew, at his observation post, started to warn his sisters.

Sarahannah's attention was drawn back to the new neighbor the other way down the road. Sasha nearly jumped when she turned also. The man with the white beard was standing at the end of his driveway, hands on his hips, looking at them. He said nothing, but with a kindly wave to the children, turned back up his driveway and ambled back inside.

"Mommy wouldn't let us open our presents. I wonder if Jessie will get to open hers," said Sarahannah.

"We should go find out," suggested Sasha.

The girls walked across their lawn, next to the road. When they reached the edge of their property, they stopped. The loquat tree marked the frontier of their expeditions. By parental fiat, they were not permitted to explore beyond that boundary on their own. They were obedient children, and conditioning simply called them to halt in their tracks. But this wasn't a natural barrier, like a river. And Sarahannah could see past, or through, such manmade limits.

"You guys aren't allowed to go over there on your own," Matthew reminded them.

"We should ask Mommy first, Sarahannah," agreed Sasha.

"But she might not let us go, and then we might not ever find out about the presents, Sashie," argued Sarahannah. "Let's go and then we'll come right back."

"Promise, Sissy?" asked Sasha.

"Promise."

They took a breath and ventured toward Jessica's house. Holding Nicholas' hand, Matthew waited at the border. After stepping along the curb in front of the next three houses, the girls stopped before crossing the street. Carefully following instructions, Sarahannah ostentatiously checked up and down the street before deciding it was clear. Few cars drove through this part of the community, in the back of the neighborhood with no real place for any stranger to drive. The girls flitted across the street and were soon knocking at their friend's front door.

Time passed. No one answered.

Sasha felt the need to state the obvious. "She's got to be there! We saw her go inside!"

Still on the family property, Matthew hollered across the street, "Girls! I think Mommy's coming! She is probably coming out here!"

Sarahannah knocked a second time, and this time, almost instantly the big door swung open. It was Jessica's Mom. She looked flustered and a little cross, but kept up the polite formalities of neighbor-parents.

"Hello, girls."

"Can Jessie come out and play?" asked Sarahannah in her most innocent voice.

"Not right now, honey. She is grounded for a little while. But I'll tell her you came by and have her visit you when she's free. Okay?"

"Okay," the girls replied, together. But before Jessica's Mom could go, Sasha impulsively asked, "Did Jessica get a present from the new man down the street?"

The older woman's eyes darkened. Her voice was not unkind, but the words were quite hard.

"I think all of you kids should stay very far away from that man. Do not take presents from strangers!" Then she shut the door.

The girls turned around to go. That not only meant facing their home, but in the far distance, the new neighbor's home as well. As unremarkable as the house was, merely a brick and cedar ranch surrounded by scraggly bushes and thin trees, it evoked a sense of wonder in the sisters when they considered who might be dwelling within. The warning they had just received only served to whet their appetite.

The girls recrossed the street and headed towards home. Their attention remained on the newcomer's place. They said nothing, each lost in her own thoughts about the man inside.

Then he stepped outside.

Sarahannah and Sasha both jumped, literally, upon seeing the imaginary man become real. He walked steadily down his driveway to the road, but amazingly, his eyes were on them.

They felt nervous, but strangely happy and secure in his steady gaze. His bushy white beard ensconced a wide, hardy smile that drew them in. He wore work pants with suspenders over a white shirt with the sleeves rolled up. Despite the abundance of facial hair, he was smoothly bald on top. He stopped and waited at his mailbox.

Matthew, the keen observer, noticed the man also. He and Nicholas joined the girls as they walked straight past their home and approached the man who had moved in two doors down.

He said nothing, appraising them from three feet above with his sparkling eyes. The children stood before him, looking up. Matthew analyzed the man's features. Sarahannah was shyly silent. But Sasha was very curious--and forward.

"Are you Santa Claus?" she demanded.

The man laughed, heartily, until his face turned red and he doubled over, steadying himself against his mailbox.

"Santa Claus! Where did you get that idea, my friend?" The man had an undistinguishable European accent, lilting and pleasing to the ears.

"You look like him," Sasha replied, matter of fact.

"And you had presents for us," added Matthew.

The man pulled at his beard thoughtfully.

"That is true, little ones. But that doesn't make one Santa Claus. And of course, Santa lives at the North Pole, doesn't he? This is quite far from there," he pointed out, looking up and to the right.

"Yes," Matthew answered. "But you had his bag!"

"His bag? You mean my duffel bag? You are very observant, Matthew. That's simply a gift from an old friend. I've been carrying it with me for years. But I find that it had kept its sturdiness and value throughout the years."

Sarahannah remembered her manners.

"We wanted to welcome you to the neighborhood." She pointed back towards home. "We live over there. My Mom says she's going to bake a pie for you"

"Thank you, Sarahannah, tell her that is very kind. I love a good apple pie, especially with the cinnamon topping!"

All three smiled at the thought, broken quickly by the sound of Mommy's voice behind them. She briskly walked towards them, with a worried look on her face.

"Sarahannah! Sasha! Matthew! Nicholas! Why are you outside of our yard?"

Busted. The children couldn't explain everything to Mommy, not there. But Mommy couldn't chastise them much, either, in front of the stranger.

"Oh, but Mrs. Warren, they were only entertaining me. They are charming girls, and such fine, smart sons," he added, winking at Matthew and Nicholas.

"Yes, they are charming... when they remember to listen to their Mommy," she answered with a look to the older children and a smile to him. "I'm sorry if they troubled you. Welcome to the neighborhood. Is there anything we can do to help you settle in to your new home?"

"Ah, there is only one thing. Your daughter mentioned something about an apple pie, and I am just old enough to discard the niceties in favor of the promise of your delicious dessert."

They laughed. "I wonder what else they may have promised you. But yes, I do hope to be baking this week."

"Thank you so much for your generosity," he winked.

With that, Mommy herded the children back home, all three with long looks back over their shoulders to the bearded man who motionlessly watched them until they disappeared into their house.

Inside, Mommy wondered about the man. Although he was a stranger, she felt an immediate warmth about his shining eyes, his open face, his air of peacefulness and apparent culture; and yes, even his resemblance to a certain person.

"Santa Claus! Santa Claus!" hollered Nicholas, finally finding his voice. "Santa Claus! Santa Claus!" Nicholas ran around the room.

"No Nicky. Just a nice man."

Mommy turned her attention to Sarahannah and Sasha. "Girls, you shouldn't promise things to strangers."

"But Mommy, he's not a stranger. He gave us presents!" argued Sasha.

"That doesn't make him a friend, at least not right away. Why do you think he brought the presents?" asked Mommy.

Trapped, Sasha paused for a moment, then blamed Sarahannah.

"Sissy made me do it! She told me to go over there!"

Sarahannah began hollering her own defense. Matthew tried to intervene, but soon, their voices easily cancelled one another out.

When Mommy got control, she managed to get a semblance of the story of the children's earlier visit to the neighbor. Mommy was not happy.

"So that makes two times today you children have wandered off our property, against our rules. I don't want you going outside again today."

"Oh Mommy..." started Sarahannah, but Mommy's look was law, so she decided against further argument.

Instead, Sarahannah turned thoughtful as Mommy started to clear the table.

"Mommy? How did that man know our names?"

Mommy couldn't answer that one. And she realized he had known her name as well.

The children got over the wonder of that question much more quickly than their Mother. They turned their attention to playtime in their bedrooms.

As the sun began to drop, a pair

of headlights flashed into the driveway.

"Daddy's home!" shouted Sasha. The children rushed to the door expectantly.

"Daddy, Daddy," they shouted, jumping into his arms when he entered, overwhelming the briefcase and newspaper in his arms. It only took a moment for Nicholas to recall the day's events and start shouting "Santa! Santa! Santa!"

"What's this?" Daddy asked. "You want me to be Santa for you? Hey kids, I can only afford to do that once a year," he winked at his wife.

"We've had an exciting day," Mommy explained drily. "A new family moved in down the street and the girls have already been over there. Without my knowing," she said with a frown meant to motivate Daddy to reinforce the rules.

He missed it. "Was it Jules?" Daddy asked her.

"Jules? Who's that?" she replied.

"You might not have met him. He actually travels quite a bit around the world for a European exporter. We've done a lot of business with him at the different branches I've worked at around the country. I had thought over the years you might have met him at the office or at a work-related dinner or something."

"Can't say that I remember him," answered his wife. She lowered her voice. "But he could be one of the, er, representatives of the Big Guy who comes once a year," she said to Daddy with a wink. "That would explain how he knew our names," she said with a little relief in her voice. "I was a little worried about a stranger knowing too much about our children."

"Well, his name is Jules Nisse," explained Daddy. "I never can pronounce that name right. He's here for an extended assignment and wanted a homier place to stay than a hotel, so he rented that house. And yes, I guess we may be hearing from him in a different way if he is the 'representative' you mentioned."

"I'm baking a pie for him." Mommy said.

Daddy flashed a hungry smile.

"Good! It's the least we can do considering the gifts he brought for the kids. He said he'd bring them by today."

"The kids seemed to think they were from him," Mommy replied. "The gifts were left on the doorstep this afternoon."

"I told you so, Mommy," Sasha couldn't resist.

Mommy ignored her. "Should they open them?"

"Sure," answered Daddy. I don't think they were meant for any special occasion."

"Yay!" the children shouted. They had heard their parents' conversation, but didn't grasp the meaning of the "Big Guy's representative." They swarmed over the gifts, and the wrapping paper didn't last long. In scant moments, they had torn into the packages and removed four intricately-designed toys.

"A train engine!" exclaimed Sarahannah.

"A dress-up doll!" shouted Sasha.

"A Nutcracker!" announced Matthew.

"A pirepighter truck!" hollered Nicholas, still confusing his consonants.

"Those are beautiful," Mommy marveled.

"You sure don't see toys like those very much anymore," observed Daddy, admiringly handling the fire truck.

"Daddy! Daddy! Pirepighter! Pirepighter!" shouted Nicky, grasping at the toy. Daddy handed it back and the girls ran into their room to play.

Seated on the living room carpet, Nicholas examined every inch of his new toy. He enjoyed taking things apart, and picked and pulled at the joints and connections in the fire truck. It was put together well, with great care and sturdiness. For a few moments that frustrated the small boy, and he started to slap at it. Then, however, he felt a sense of satisfaction and security: this toy would not break.

Meanwhile, Matthew climbed up on to his Daddy's lap. "What is the man's name again?" he started.

"Mr. Jules. I work with him fairly often," Daddy replied.

"He looks a lot like Santa Claus. And he brought us presents. Could he be Santa Claus?" Matthew tried.

"Well, it's not exactly Christmas right now, is it?" answered his Dad. "I think he is a work client who is trying to be nice to a friend and his family."

That stopped Matt for a moment. "So, you are friends with Santa," he concluded.

Daddy chuckled briefly. "No, no, Matty. I'm friends with Mr. Jules. You know, our new neighbor."

But names didn't mean much to Matthew. He had carefully analyzed the data and come to his own conclusion.

Dinner came and went, and then it was time for bed. After the day's adventures the children felt exceptionally drowsy. Nicholas immediately fell asleep in his toddler bed, still lovingly clutching his new fire truck. Matthew carefully placed his Nutcracker on top of the dresser--out of the reach of his younger brother. The girls shuffled off to their bunk beds, and were tucked in with a kiss and a prayer by their parents.

As the door closed, Sasha whispered from the lower bunk, "Sissy, do you think he's Santa Claus?"

"I don't know," answered Sarahannah. "Daddy says his name is Mr. Jewel. Can Santa have two names?"

"I guess so," replied Sasha, yawning. "What about 'Kris Kringle?'"

"That's true," affirmed Sarahannah turning over and pulling up the blanket around her cheek. "I hope it is Santa," she murmured, and then it was dark.

The next morning after breakfast, the children rushed outside to try to catch a glimpse of the man their parents instructed them to call "Mr. Jules." They stopped at the hedge, and were just in time to see the old red pickup truck back out of his driveway and pull away in the other direction.

"Where is he going?" asked Sasha.

"He must be going to work," answered Matthew. "Daddy left a little while ago."

"Won't he be late?"

"I guess he will if he doesn't hurry!" Sarahannah observed.

"Maybe he knows a special shortcut," Sasha considered.

The day passed slowly. Sarahannah decided to water her sunflowers, which had sprouted but didn't grow fast enough for the children. First she had to shoo away Nicholas, who insisted on using the hose like a pirepighter every chance he had. After he watered some grass, a squirrel, the air, Matthew, a toy car, and a tree, Sarahannah coaxed control of the hose back from him.

"Hurry up!" Sarahannah quietly demanded of the flowers as she drenched them. "I'm not sure you guys will ever grow up to be real sunflowers."

Jessica came over to play, and the children ran off to the backyard. Their friend described how she got into trouble with her Mother.

"I got a Christmas present from the new neighbor who lives down the street. My Mom said it was bad for me to talk to a stranger. I told her he wasn't, because he knew my name. It was on a nametag on the present!"

"Maybe he works with your Daddy, like he does with ours," suggested Sasha.

"I don't know. But Mom says I can't go over there anymore."

Sasha asked, "What was in your present?"

"A bell for my bike. Mommy says it's for letting her know where I'm at."

"Santa Claus! Santa! Santa!" Nicholas chanted. It had swiftly become his favorite word.

That turned Sarahannah's thoughts to the real question on her mind. "Do you think he's Santa Claus?"

"That man? No way! I don't even think he looks like Santa," answered Jessica.

The next three days, including the weekend, were drenched in rain. The children could only gather on the living room couch and stare out through the picture window. There was little activity in the neighborhood, however, except the occasional car splashing through the water. The children couldn't see Mr. Jules' house because of the sharp angle and the big hedge on the side of their driveway.

First Sarahannah, then Sasha and Matthew drifted away from the window. Nicholas remained, perhaps tired and ready for a nap. He watched the rain fall steadily, the only movement now in the street. Leaning his full body against the couch, chin resting on the top of the cushion, his eyes felt drowsy. He clutched his favorite blanket, and might have actually fallen asleep--had he not seen the reindeer.

It was just one animal, majestic and entirely out of place, trotting purposefully down the middle of the road. Nicholas could tell by its antlers-- they didn't move back and forth in search of something--that the animal was keeping its gaze focused on a spot down the street. It was clearly intent on reaching its destination, despite the pouring rain. Nicholas wasn't sure if this was unusual. In his three years and four months he had never seen a reindeer before, but why wouldn't one just happen by, like a lost dog or a neighborhood squirrel? He gazed after the reindeer until it trotted out of sight. And then he fell asleep, head down on the top of the couch.

The inclement weather kept the children's attention away from Mr. Jules. Instead, their thoughts drifted to other channels. A trip to the mall and the movies, Sunday School, and brunch at a restaurant helped pass the time while the rain poured down.

Monday morning, however, dawned cloudless. A slight misty fog told of a bright sun already busy evaporating the remaining humidity in the ground and the atmosphere.

Free from the confines of their home, the children burst outdoors and simply rode their bikes in circles for a few minutes. That wore off some of their pent-up energy. After inspecting her still-stunted sunflowers, Sarahannah suggested a game of freeze tag. This always began by nominating Sasha for the key role.

"You're 'it'!" Sarahannah laughed, and ran away. Matthew backed up to a safe distance, ready to play.

"I'm always 'it'!" argued Sasha. "Why do I always have to chase you? I don't want to!"

Sarahannah was already halfway across the yard. Nick hadn't moved anywhere. He still didn't get the concept of freeze tag, not quite yet.

"Oh, all right, let's do something else," Sarahannah answered.

"Let's play ball toss," Matthew offered. "I'll get the blue ball." He ran into garage and emerged with a foam rubber ball. His first throw was a good one to Sarahannah. Still a little upset at not getting her way with the game of freeze tag, she intentionally threw the ball high and hard in Sasha's direction. "Here, catch!"

The ball sailed over Sasha's head, past the hedge and into Mr. Phillips' front yard next door. The children rushed to the hedge to see what became of it.

"Now you've done it, Sissy!" challenged Sasha. "It's rolling into the street!"

Hurrying down the driveway to the road, the children saw the ball slowly come to rest along the curb at the far end of Mr. Phillips' property. Looking carefully both ways for cars, they edged down the street along the curb to retrieve the ball.

"I'll get it!" Sasha cried, trying to push her way past Sarahannah.

"No! You hold Nick's hand," commanded her older sister.

They approached the ball. As Sarahannah bent down to pick it up, she stopped.

"What's the matter Sissy?" asked Sasha.

She remained still.

"Sissy?"

Sarahannah straightened up and stared at Mr. Jules' house.

"They go there," she said.

"What? What go there?" Sasha wondered.

"All these footprints," Sarahannah answered.

Matthew and Sasha looked. Sure enough, there were dozens of prints in the still-moist ground. They weren't footprints, really, because they were made by hooves.

"A lot of very big animals must have done this," said Sarahannah.

Sasha ventured, "Like a bear, you mean?"

"Bears have paws. This is like a

horse! Who would ride horses to Mr. Jules' house?"

"These don't look like the horseshoe Daddy keeps in the garage," Sasha added.

They fell silent until Nicholas suddenly had an idea.

"Rudolph!" he exclaimed. "Santa Rudolph!"

The kids looked at each other and then at the markings. They were indeed the hoof prints of several reindeer.

The children's thoughts returned to the mystery of Jules Nisse. The rest of the day was filled with conjecture, suppositions, and speculation. It only ended when they were tucked in for bed.

"Good night, sweetheart," said Mommy, kissing Sarahannah.

"Mommy?"

"Yes, honey."

"Will Santa Claus come again this year?"

Mommy looked at her with a strange look in her eyes.

"Of course! He comes every year, Sarahannah. Is something the matter?"

"Well," she answered slowly, "I was afraid that since we moved again maybe he might not find us."

"You have nothing to worry about, honey. Do you remember how we filled out change of address forms for our mail? That works for Santa, too. He knows where we live."

"But doesn't everything change? Maybe he'll just stop bringing toys." Her bottom lip quivered in a prelude to a tired cry.

Mommy hugged her. "Some things don't change, like how the sun comes up every morning and how your Daddy eats Lucky Charms for breakfast every day and how there's church every Sunday. And most importantly, how much we love you."

Sarahannah was warmed by the words, and the hug. A little reassurance went a long way with her.

"By the way," Mommy wondered, "Why do you ask now, six months away from Christmas?"

"I just want to behave better. I want to be extra good for him," explained Sarahannah.

"Oh, you are already a wonderful little girl," assured Mommy, giving her a tight squeeze. "Now go to sleep. And if you want to be extra wonderful, tomorrow you can help me clean the bathroom."

The mere thought of that chore made Sarahannah tired. Scrubbing the toilet with that ugly brush and smelly chemicals was not pleasant. She rolled over and resolved to behave better, but perhaps not to the level of "extra wonderful." Soon she was fast asleep.

3

Nicholas loved his toddler bed. It was much more than a functional place to sleep. It was designed to resemble a fire truck complete with a light on top, and inside he felt secure and comfortable, surrounded by curtains of soft blankets and mounds of stuffed animals. There was even room for his new toy fire truck. In this place, he was almost always perfectly content--like a permanent embrace from his Mommy. But laying there this night, he realized that something had awakened him. It was dark outside; definitely "night-night time." Matthew was snoring loudly and regularly in his bed across the room. That noise was very familiar to Nicholas. But there had been another that had pierced his unconsciousness and he awoke. Then he heard it again--the sound of small bells jingling. Given the circumstances of the past few days, this was enough to stir Nick to clamber over the side of his sanctuary and venture out.

When Sarahannah awoke, the house was still. She wondered why she was awake. Then she heard a shuffling noise and her heartbeat quickened. The bedroom door opened and Nicholas stood in the doorway.

"Santa, Sissy! Santa!" he called in a night-time stage whisper.

Sarahannah blinked. "What's the matter, Nicky?" she asked, using a little child voice for her young brother.

"Santa! See?" He pointed to the living room. There was a cool, bluish glow emanating from the front of the house. Sarahannah thought it was rather bright outside for the middle of the night.

Matthew appeared, which was even stranger than seeing Nicholas there. The older boy was such a sound sleeper that only something very important could have moved him.

"It is Santa, Sarahannah," he announced. His manner was more solemn than excited. "I went up front and looked. He's there."

Now Sasha stirred in the lower bunk. "What's going on?" she asked, dreamily.

"Nicholas and Matthew saw something out front." Sarahannah

couldn't quite grasp the concept of what her brothers were telling her.

"Santa!   Santa!"   Nicholas insisted.

"I'm going to get Daddy," said Sarahannah.

"I'm going to see Santa!" Sasha exclaimed, racing out of bed, through the house and into the living room. Matthew ran with her and Nick toddled along behind. Sarahannah thought for a moment, then ran to the front, also.

She caught up with Nicholas and held his hand as they caught up with the twins, standing together peering out over the sill of the big picture window that faced the front lawn. They were standing quite still, in quiet awe. Sarahannah moved forward, slowly, with a premonition that something incredible was about to happen.

And it did.

The first thing they noticed was the snow. Snow? In the middle of summer? But there it was. Light flakes drifted down, despite a clear night sky. The ground and trees and cars were all covered with white. Under the moon, the night scene glowed bluishly into their living room. But, *it's July*, thought Sarahannah.   The younger children seemed to accept the scene without question.

Those thoughts were fleeting. For, as their eyesight focused out of doors, the children saw milling about on the snow-covered street, eight reindeer harnessed to a sleigh. A red, beat-up sleigh, dented and rusted in spots. One that, had the children heard of the old television program, would have seemed eerily equivalent to the pickup truck in *Sanford and Son*.

"Ohhhh, look everybody!" exclaimed Sasha.

A man dressed in red, trimmed in luxuriant white cotton, was bent over, fastening a strap of bells to the harness on the far side of the sleigh. Finishing, he stood up and gently chatted with the reindeer as he moved forward. Coming around the front of the team, the man turned and fixed his gaze straight into the picture window of the children's' home. All but Nicholas stepped back involuntarily, as if they had been caught spying. But the penetratingly warm and welcome smile on Jules Nisse's face beckoned them to come outside.

They did, as in a dream. Barefooted, in their pajamas, the children did not feel the snow or cold.

Quietly, in awe, they approached the great man. Once more he silently appraised them from three feet above their heads as they stood before him, looking up.

"Would you like to go for a ride?" he simply asked.

Matthew, who had been admiring the construction of the sleigh, silently stepped forward first. They all then climbed aboard in a daze, squeezing together on the single bench seat in the front of the sleigh. Jules joined them, fastening a strap around their waists that acted as a seatbelt, and covered their laps with a wool blanket. Before starting, he fixed them with his merry gaze.

"Do you...believe?" he asked.

"Yes!" the children shouted together, with Nicholas echoing a half-beat behind.

"You are Santa Claus!" Sasha managed to gasp, happily. "I knew it!"

Jules whipped up the reindeer, and as they jerked the sleigh forward, answered, "No, my dear. But I'll tell you all about it!" He laughed as the sleigh slid along the road, and smoothly glided into the air.

The children were not startled by

the ride. In fact, it was precisely as they had privately imagined a ride in Santa's sleigh. They stared at their neighborhood from a new vantage point, looking from above down on to the roofs of the homes along their street.

They rose higher into the air, past the end of the street, over the houses and streetlamps and treetops. From high above, Nicholas saw a fire truck race off to an emergency, lights flashing. Its tiny size reminded him of his new toy.

Sasha noticed how clear the stars looked above the lights of her neighborhood. This was so exciting, she burst out in a gleeful chorus of "Jingle Bells," causing everyone to laugh heartily. It was a crisply clear night, but despite the falling snow, no clouds appeared.

Sarahannah glanced into the back of the sleigh. A dark storage area stood empty.

"What are we doing?" Sarahannah asked. "There aren't any toys in the back." She had to speak loudly, for the wind whistled through their hair.

"This is what our office refers as 'Reconnoitering,' Sarahannah," answered Jules, also having to speak up to be heard. "You may be familiar with the phrase, 'He's making a list, he's checking it twice, he's going to find out who's naughty or nice?' This is how we do it throughout the year."

That made Sasha want to launch into another song, but instead she asked, "'We?' If you're not Santa, who are you? Where is he?"

"There are many of us, my dear. Hold the railing for a moment," he warned. Jules maneuvered the reins, guiding the reindeer into a sloping right turn. They headed to the edge of town and started to descend down another snow-covered residential street, this one called "Sycamore Road."

Jules laughed as he considered Sasha's question. "You are the curious one, aren't you? But full of courageous faith.

"Think of me as one of Santa's helpers, even though I'm not an elf. I'm kind of a 'regional Santa,' you might say. Sometimes I even portray him at the shopping mall, depending on my assignment. This year, however, I am compiling the 'Naughty or Nice' list for this state."

The twins looked at each other,

realizing they too could be the object of his observation. And they hadn't exactly shunned "naughtiness" as much as they might have. Sarahannah recalled how she had vacillated over being "extra wonderful," and winced.

The sleigh flew on through the perfectly-still night sky. Tiny stars lit the heavens like a tapestry.

"So, where are we going?" Sasha tried.

Jules pointed to a clump of homes off to the northwest. "We're almost there. Keep your arms inside the sleigh and hold the strap, for the landings can be bumpy."

The sleigh touched down, with the reindeer working hard to slow down their momentum in the snow. Soon they had stopped in front of a two story red brick colonial home.

Smoke from the chimney signaled a working fireplace. Just the smell of the burning wood was warmth itself. Sarahannah looked at the chimney expectantly, thinking it the suitable entry for someone who controlled a sleigh powered by flying reindeer.

Jules followed Sarahannah's gaze.

"No, I do not enter the home through the chimney, my dear," he smiled. "There's a much simpler way to get inside. I will show you. Come with me."

The children carefully folded away their blanket, unstrapped themselves, and clambered down from the sleigh. Nicholas almost fell in the snow trying to get his "ground" legs back after the unusual ride through the skies they had just experienced, but Matthew helped him up and held his hand.

"Stay along the curb this time-- don't play in the thoroughfare!" Jules called back to the reindeer in his unusual accent and cadence.

"They like to wander on to the front garden if I fail to be strict with them," he confided to the children as they approached the house.

Led by Jules, the group mounted the porch and gathered at a beautiful double front door. Jules rang the illuminated doorbell, positioned three feet below the house number, 822.

The children weren't sure what to expect. This was not like entering the house in the way they imagined Santa would do it. Sasha grabbed Jules' hand, and Nicholas grasped his suit coat as Matthew stepped back. Sarahannah hid behind Jules' leg.

A woman in heavy makeup and hairspray answered the door. She was dressed very nicely, the children thought, as if she was going to a party. She wore a pearl necklace and was fussy.

"Mr. Nisse! Thank you for coming. How nice! Thank you, come in, come in! I've been looking forward to meeting you. And you have some little friends with you! I'll go get my husband. And," she offered, glancing at the children, "I happen to have some hot chocolate warming on the stove."

"Thank you, Mrs. Nelson," answered Jules. "We will wait in your front room."

Jules and the children stepped into a showroom that looked to be straight out of a home decor magazine.

"Wait!" Sasha called, realizing how antiseptically clean everything was in the house. "We didn't wipe our feet!"

Yet, despite the snow, they had not tracked in any trace of the inclement weather. Their feet were dry--and still warm.

Soon, Mr. Nelson joined them in the front room. He wore a very short haircut, almost like a soldier, Matthew thought. He wore slacks and a cardigan and a wide, smiling face that seemed a tad troubled. The men shook hands and everyone sat down.

"Mr. Nelson, this is Sarahannah, Sasha, Matthew, and Nicholas--a name I love!" laughed Jules. They are making the rounds with me tonight as observers."

"Very nice to have you," Mr. Nelson addressed the children.

Mrs. Nelson brought in mugs of hot chocolate, which felt perfect on a cold winters' night.

Glancing at the children as they enjoyed their hot refreshment, Mr. Nelson suggested to Jules, "They needed a little dose of reality, eh?"

"Indeed, Mr. Nelson. Speaking of which, about your two boys... ."

"We're glad you're here, Mr. Nisse," said Mr. Nelson, pushing his reading glasses to the top of his head. "Our twins have been pretty rambunctious lately, but overall I don't think they've been all that bad." Twins? Sasha and Matthew involuntarily glanced at one another. Mr. Nelson continued. "When it's so many months away from Christmas, it's difficult to get the boys to behave by reminding them that Santa and his presents may not come."

"Two boys, ah yes," answered Jules, looking down. "Ricky and David? Their behavior file shows that they paid attention in school but Ricky sometimes sings aloud in class, distracting the other children."

"Well, he does have a nice voice. But their teacher keeps them separated in school, and says that seems to help," replied Mrs. Nelson.

"Let's take a look then, shall we?"

Everyone set down their mugs. Led by the Nelson parents, Jules moved down a long hall and to the doorway of what looked like a large playroom. It was filled with toys, games, stuffed animals, and sports equipment. The three adults crowded into the doorway but went no further, and they gazed silently into the room for a long time. They seemed to be observing some activity inside the room, but it was difficult for the children to see through so many legs in such a small space.

Mrs. Nelson said something, and then they heard a boy's voice. Sarahannah judged him to be about her age, maybe a little younger. She heard him say, innocently enough, "Oh hi, Mom. We weren't doing anything. Just playing."

The parents turned away, leaving Jules to gauge things in the doorway by himself. The children could see much more clearly now. They saw two young boys at opposite ends of the room, kneeling behind a thick array of toy soldiers and artillery. Playing the role of two generals, the boys muttered incoherent threats to each other and then started throwing some of the toys at each other. They seemed utterly oblivious to the guests at the door--as if they weren't there. But Jules paid close attention to them.

Eventually one boy managed to hit the other with a building block that had been part of his army's fort. The stricken general ventured forth to slug back with his hand. Both started crying for their parents while struggling over a toy tank.

The boys' father finally re-appeared to intervene, and Jules turned away to consult with Mrs. Nelson once more in the living room.

"Naughty," he sighed, taking out an electronic notebook and making two notations.

"They've been like this for a month," answered Mrs. Nelson, distractedly. "Fighting, fighting,

fighting."

"Perhaps they need a little more parental attention. But that is not for me to say," replied Jules. "Someone will check back with you towards the end of the year. You could," he added, "remind them of our policy about coal in their stockings if they maintain this kind of behavior."

"Of course, Mr. Nisse. Thank you so much for checking in. I know how busy you must be. Ricky and David may not get all the Christmas presents they want this year! But this is a great reality check."

"Naturally, that's out of my hands," responded Jules. "But I hope you are able to see the importance of proper parenting in shaping their behavior."

"Yes indeed, yes indeed," Mrs. Nelson fussed. "Thank you, thank you."

Mr. Nelson returned from the playroom, looking a little worried.

"They're on the "Naughty" list, aren't they?"

"Yes," Jules answered simply.

"Yes, well, good. Very good. They may have to learn the hard way this year that Santa doesn't reward naughty children with nice presents,"

Mr. Nelson said, as much to himself as the visitors. "Here is a printout of the record of their behavior since last Christmas, one for each of the boys." He handed over two forms that, to the children, seemed to be thoroughly covered with notations by the Nelsons. "It's actually not as bad as you might think, considering their behavior tonight."

There was a thump and a scream from a room upstairs. Two voices starting crying again.

"Um, yes, I'm sure. Thank you, indeed," murmured Jules. "I must move on. As a note of encouragement," he added, "allow me to remind you that this is precisely why we check the list at least twice, rather than only once. It is for quality control, shall we say, to ensure that each child is fairly judged. Therefore, the young Masters Nelson will have a second chance to show their true Christmas spirit."

"Oh yes. And we absolutely support your recommendations," Mr. Nelson responded. "It might not hurt them to find a lump of West Virginia coal in their stocking one Christmas morning." He seemed a little exasperated.

"And so it may be. But allow my friends and I to depart now, for there are a great many other stops on our trek this evening," answered Jules. "I wish you all a good night."

Everyone stood up and Jules led the way out the door and into the night. The children--even little Nicholas--had been wonderfully silent while watching to proceedings, taking in the meaning of it all.

"You really do find out how kids are behaving? All kids?" asked Sarahannah as they approached the sleigh. She thought of her own transgressions and became worried.

"Yes, all children," responded Jules in a matter-of-fact manner, while loading the children onboard.

"I believe you," Sasha said, fervently.

They lifted off again, high and silent into the night. Now the ride wasn't quite as exhilarating for the children. Sarahannah and Sasha contemplated their own shortcomings, and found themselves a bit lacking. They silently considered their Christmas reward, whatever it might be. Little Nicholas was in awe of all of the proceedings. Matthew, though, was consumed by the wonders of reindeer-powered flight, and the design of the sleigh.

"How does this thing fly?" he asked.

"You'll have to ask the engineers," responded Jules, eyes locked straight forward--but with a glimmer of a grin.

"Who are they?" tried Matt. "Are they elves?"

"Oh, just some colleagues who work for my firm."

"Does my Daddy work with them, like he works with you?"

"No, he does not," responded Jules, shutting down that line of questioning. Instead, as they flew on, he gave the children time to contemplate the amazing things that had confronted them this night.

"Did those boys at that house even see us?" asked Sasha, finally.

"No," Jules replied frankly. "They had no idea we were there. And that's as it should be," he added. "I would not be able to develop a proper 'Naughty or Nice' recommendation when they come to sit on my lap at the shopping center. There, they place their orders, pose for pictures, and in three minutes are gone." That triggered a memory for Sarahannah.

"Did we ever see you at the shopping center?" she wondered.

"You did, my dear."

"When?" asked Sasha.

"Let's see. It was in another state. You and Matthew were very small and Sarahannah was three years old. She asked for a 'Tickle Me Elmo' toy. And as for you," he added mischievously, "your diaper was wet."

It took a moment for that to sink in. Sasha started at the thought and blushed. Matthew laughed.

Jules Nisse guided the reindeer back down into another neighborhood, this one quite well-to-do. The houses were larger, and set farther apart, like miniature estates rather than mere homes. But they were all constructed on the same modern design of multiple gables and roofs, and sided with brown brick. To Sasha, that made them look like oversize anthills. Jules parked the sleigh and they approached the porch of one of the anthills. Nicholas noticed something funny about one of the upstairs windows. He pointed.

"That window looks like it's broken," Matthew observed.

"It appears that it does have a

hole in it," Jules replied, evenly, almost knowingly. He rang the doorbell.

"Mr. Nisse," exclaimed the homeowner at the door, pulling a pipe from his smiling mouth. "Is it that time again?"

"Ah yes, Dr. Huxtable. Such a pleasure to see you again," replied Jules.

They entered an oversized entryway with a cathedral ceiling.

"You've got some friends with you," the man observed. "Hello children. Have a seat here in the living room. My little girl and I were making some funny hats out of construction paper in the kitchen. Do you want to wear one?"

"No thank you," Sarahannah politely but shyly answered for her brothers and sister.

"Can I get you something to drink? Or a snack? Pudding?"

"No thank you," Sarahannah repeated.

"But Sissy, I'd like some--" started Sasha, but her older sister quick kicked her in the shin. "Never mind," she finished, pained. She turned to Sarahannah. "Stop bossing me, Sissy," she hissed.

"Hmm. Looks like a little sibling

rivalry already," Dr. Huxtable offered.

"They are observing this evening. And hopefully acquiring some things to think about," responded Jules pointedly. "But we are here to discuss your children, Theo, Vanessa, and, let's see...Rudy."

"Let me get to my laptop and I'll get your behavior record for them. My wife has a late night at the law office, so it's just me and the kids tonight. They are watching TV in the family room. You know where it's at," Dr. Huxtable waived them down a long hallway.

Jules Nisse seemed much larger in the confines of the hallway, and the children crowded along behind him. As in the first home, he stopped at the doorway to observe. Apparently, they were again invisible to the room's occupants.

Once more it wasn't easy for any of the children to see, but Sasha had the best vantage point this time, squeezing in next to one of Jules' legs. She saw two girls and a boy, two of them plainly older than Sarahannah but one about her age, watching a sitcom rerun. Sasha didn't know if "Theo" or "Rudy" was the boy, but the older girl was talking.

"...those boys to help you with

that. They shouldn't have run away when the ball went through it. You didn't do it!"

"Yeah, but Sis, I got to pay up because Dad told us not to play near the house." He looked glum. "Gonna take me a long time to save enough money to fix that window. I'll be delivering a lot of newspapers!"

"I told you so, you should have listened to me!" the smallest child piped up.

"You don't have to rub it in, Rudy," the boy replied.

"You can have my allowance, if Dad remembers it this week. Will that help?" Rudy said.

Jules began to turn around from the room, and the children had to scramble in the thin hallway to allow him to move back through it. Like ducklings trailing their mother they followed him back into the living room. Sarahannah thought she heard Mr. Jules muttering something to himself about a "too perfect sitcom family" but he cut it short when they entered the living room.

Dr. Huxtable was waiting for them.

"Here you go," he offered three reports to Jules. "Any questions?"

Jules replied thoughtfully, "As a middle child, does Vanessa try too hard to be like her grown up sisters? Does she...no longer believe?"

"Oh she starts to doubt from time to time," answered Dr. Huxtable. He smiled slyly. "But I believe. And that's usually good enough for her. She's still Daddy's Little Girl."

"Very well. Thank you and give my best wishes to Clair. So sorry we missed her."

They walked to the door.

"We'll be checking in again later in the year," Jules said as they shook hands.

"See you later, kids. Maybe we can make hats next time," smiled Dr. Huxtable.

"I still wish I could have had some pudding," grumbled Sasha.

"C'mon, Sashie," Sarahannah said as she pulled her sister out the door and back into the night.

Noticing something outside, Jules suddenly moved faster than usual, leaving the children a few steps behind. "Reindeer!" he commanded.

Sure enough, they had wandered onto the front yard, milling around, trying to poke through the snow looking for grass.

"Blitzen! Donder! All of you! Away from there!"

Jules coaxed them back on to the street before boarding the children.

As they flew off once more, Sarahannah turned to Jules.

"That boy played baseball in the yard. That was wrong."

"That is correct."

"But it sounded like somebody else broke the window with a ball. Why did he say he did it?"

"He took responsibility, my dear. If he hadn't allowed the game to be played so close to the house, the ball would not have hit the window. He is going to have to pay to repair the window. But," Jules added, "He has most definitely earned a place on the 'Nice' list."

As they coasted through the snowy night sky, Sarahannah turned to her sister.

"Sashie, I'm sorry about kicking you. I will try not to boss you anymore."

Sasha smiled. "Its okay, Sissy." She leaned against her older sister in a sort of half-hug.

The children and Jules Nisse flew on through the night, visiting other families throughout the town and collecting more behavior reports. Jules kept careful notes on his electronic notebook on families like the Bradys, Cleavers, Waltons, and many more. Finally, as the moon began to set in the night sky Jules leaned over to Matthew, seated next to him. "You have been admiring this sleigh since we began tonight's adventure. How would you like to drive, er, fly the vehicle?"

Startled, Matthew straightened to attention, eyes wide. All he could do was vigorously shake his head and exclaim a fervent, "Uh, huh!"

Jules grinned through his white beard and handed over the reins. There was a momentary dip in the flight as the reins slackened slightly, but Matt soon pulled them taut once more. Sasha shivered briefly and pulled the blanket up under her chin, but the sleigh steadied and they flew on. Getting the hang of it, Matthew drew the reins to the right and then to the left, putting the sleigh through some paces. He looked at Nicholas and the two boys laughed.

"Matty flies!" exclaimed Nicholas.

Matthew let his younger brother take one of the reins, while Jules carefully watched. The boys concentrated extra hard on keeping the sleigh flying on a straight line, but at one point they expertly dodged a tall television transmission tower.

Eventually, they handed the reins back to Jules, and the sleigh finally made one last expert landing in front of the children's' home. Jules undid the belt strap one last time to allow the kids to jump down onto their snow-covered lawn. Nicholas gave him a big bear hug before Jules helped him down from the sleigh.

They turned to Mr. Jules and he gave them one more quiet, searching look from three feet above.

"There is a special quality about children with such tender hearts as yours. They may bruise easily, but they are stout. And they will be true and just, an example to many others. Once you believe something, you will truly believe. And that will keep this sleigh flying."

Sarahannah wasn't exactly sure what that meant, but she understood the tone, and Mr. Jules' intent. She had one last question; one to which she thought she knew the answer, but it would be unbearable if she were wrong.

"Will you...stay...in our neighborhood?"

One last searching, smiling look from Jules Nisse.

"As long as you'll have me, I'll be two doors down," he replied.

"Thank you," she said, looking up.

"The debt is mine," he answered, whipping up the reindeer one last time. "Ho, ho, ho!" he called out as reindeer pulled the sleigh down the street towards his house. As the children made their way into their own home, they made one more surprising discovery. There, in the snow, under the bright moonlight of the clear sky, were four sunflowers standing along the east wall of the house, tall and proud.

"Girls! What in the world are you doing, sleeping in so late?" Mommy bustled about the bedroom, picking up toys and putting away clothes. "It's almost nine o'clock!"

The sun was out. They awoke, slowly. Sarahannah looked out the open window: green grass and fresh leaves could be seen and smelled. The snow was gone. Nevertheless, powerful memories of their long, magical night came pouring back to them as the mists of sleep cleared away.

Sasha nearly blurted out something, but thought better of it. Mommy left the room to get Matthew going. He was snoring far later into the morning than usual. Nicholas was awake but already content with a bottle of juice in his toddler bed.

Climbing down from the top bunk bed, Sarahannah looked at Sasha. "If other parents already know about Mr. Jules and Santa Claus, then our Mommy and Daddy do too, right?"

"Yeah!" answered Sasha. "That means they keep a report on us, I guess."

"We'll just have to keep trying to be good. But if I mess up, I'll tell you I'm sorry right now, okay?"

"Okay," replied Sasha. "Me too."

They could hear Nicky in the next room, exclaiming "Santa!" and "sleigh!" and "reindeer!" to Mommy. He made engine noises for the sleigh. Matthew began telling Mommy about a dream he had, in which he flew Santa's sleigh. The girls weren't worried that Mommy would figure out what it all really meant. Their family was there for them, to watch over them, and so was Jules Nisse. Sarahannah had learned that even if they moved again and again, to other neighborhoods in strange cities, some things would never change: the children would always be loved. And in this neighborhood at least, there was someone special, just two doors down.

The End